D1256986

Ganga
The River that Flows from Heaven to Earth

Vatsala Sperling

Illustrated by Harish Johari
and Pieter Weltevrede

Bear Cub Books
Rochester, Vermont

For Dada

Special thanks to Eliza Thomas for her editorial support

Bear Cub Books
One Park Street
Rochester, Vermont 05767
www.InnerTraditions.com

Bear Cub Books is a division of Inner Traditions International

Library of Congress Cataloging-in-Publication Data

Sperling, Vatsala, 1961–
Ganga : the river that flows from heaven to earth / Vatsala Sperling ; illustrated by Harish Johari and Pieter Weltevrede.
p. cm.
Summary: "Explains how the Hindu goddess Ganga came to Earth as the Ganges River and why millions of people today take comfort in her healing waters"—Provided by publisher.
ISBN: 978-1-59143-089-6 (hardcover)
1. Ganga (Hindu deity)—Juvenile literature. 2. Ganga (Hindu deity) 3. Mythology, Hindu. I. Johari, Harish, 1934–1999, ill. II. Weltevrede, Pieter, ill. III. Title.
BL1225.G35 S74 2008
294.5'2114 22

2008009354

Printed and bound in India by Replika Press Pvt. Ltd.

10 9 8 7 6 5 4 3 2 1

Text design and layout by Virginia Scott Bowman
This book was typeset in Berkeley with Abbess and Nueva as display typefaces

To send correspondence to the author of this book, mail a first-class letter to the author c/o Inner Traditions • Bear & Company, One Park Street, Rochester, VT 05767, and we will forward the communication.

Cast of Characters

Brahma
(Brahm-'ha)
Lord of Creation

Vishnu
('Vish-noo)
Lord of Preservation

Shiva
(Shee-'va)
Lord of Destruction

Bali
('Baah-lee)
A virtuous demon king who banished the lazy gods from Heaven

Kashyapa and Aditi
(Kahsh-ya-pa) ('Aah-dee-tee)
A virtuous sage and his wife, Lord Vishnu's earthly parents

Vamana
('Vaah-ma-na)
Lord Vishnu's incarnation on Earth as a dwarf

Shukracharya
(Shuk-'raah-'chaar-ya)
A sage who is the teacher of the demons

Ganga
(Gan-'ga)
Daughter of Lord Brahma, a river that came from Heaven to Earth

Durvasa
(Dur-'vaah-'saah)
A sage well known for his anger and terrible curses

Sagar
('Saah-gar)
A king with sixty thousand sons who wanted to rule the whole universe

Kapil
(Ka-pil)
A sage who was falsely accused of stealing King Sagar's horse

Anshuman
(An-shu-man)
King Sagar's only surviving son

Bhagirath
(Bha-'gee-raht-h)
A descendent of King Sagar whose devotion brought Ganga to the Earth as a sacred river

Janu
('Jaah-nu)
A sage who drank up the entire river Ganga

About Ganga

The Ganga (or Ganges) is a sacred and beautiful river in India that flows from the high reaches of the Himalayas, through the northern plains, and down to the Bay of Bengal. It is named after the goddess Ganga. The story of how Ganga was born, and how she became a river, tells of a journey from places even higher than the Himalayan mountaintops—a trip from the heavens themselves. Ganga's journey is a long one, with many twists and turns, filled with tales of sorrow and joy, hardship and renewed hope.

Long, long ago, the world was ruled by a powerful demon king named Bali. At first, he was disciplined and virtuous, ruling his subjects with justice and giving freely to anyone who was needy or hungry, but in time he grew as proud and arrogant as he was strong. He extended his empire to include three worlds—Earth, Heaven, and the Underworld—and even drove the gods from the heavens. He wanted to be the most powerful being in the universe.

"There are no other gods. I am the only god. Worship ME," declared Bali, and he forbade his subjects from worshipping or making offerings to any gods.

The gods, now homeless, were very unhappy. They went to Lord Brahma, the creator, asking for help. "King Bali is a menace to us all!" they cried.

The wise Brahma chided the gods gently. "You have brought this upon yourselves. I have seen you grow lazy and frivolous, while Bali has taken an oath of charity and has grown ever more virtuous and strong." The gods bowed their heads. Brahma smiled and continued. "But don't lose hope. We will go to Vishnu, and he will help you."

Vishnu Loka, Lord Vishnu's home, was set in a vast, milky sea that sustained all of Brahma's creations. The mighty five-hooded serpent, Shesha, bobbed gently on the waves. Lord Vishnu rested with his wife, the Goddess Lakshmi, upon the serpent's snug coils.

When Lord Vishnu saw the entourage of unhappy gods led by Lord Brahma, he asked, "What brings you here?" The gods fell over each other in narrating their complaints about the demon Bali.

"He drove us from our homes!"

"He doesn't let anyone worship us!"

"He is invincible!"

"Help us, please," they all begged.

Lord Vishnu looked at them and said, "King Bali follows the path of virtue and cannot be defeated in battle. But I think I know just the way to trick him. Yes . . . I will go to Earth myself. Yes . . . ," Vishnu paused thoughtfully, ". . . disguised as a dwarf." He flashed a brilliant smile, with a twinkle in his eyes. "Don't worry. The heavens will soon be yours again."

Lord Vishnu loved visiting the earth. This emerald planet that Lord Brahma had created so lovingly and filled with plants, animals, and people fascinated him. In no time at all he had chosen his new earthly parents, Sage Kashyapa and his wife, Aditi. They were very wise, very old, and very poor. Pious and reverent, they prayed each day to the gods and were delighted with their angelic baby boy—who they soon realized was the holy being Lord Vishnu himself. Truly, he was the answer to their prayers! They named their new son Vamana and raised him with care and affection. Vamana never grew tall. Even when he was all grown up he remained a dwarf.

Shukracharya, a clever demon who was a royal counselor and teacher in the court of King Bali, was also quick to recognize Vishnu in the new baby boy. He knew that Vishnu had some devious reason for being born to such poor parents. He knew that somehow Vishnu would use his parents' poverty to deceive King Bali. He went straight away to warn the king.

"Beware, King Bali," he said, "Lord Vishnu is here on Earth. He is here to win back the heavens you have conquered." Shukracharya's voice was grave. "You must watch yourself. You have gone too far in your lust for power and wealth. You must stop harassing the gods," he warned.

"And one more thing . . ." Shukracharya hesitated. How could he explain? "If a small stranger comes asking for charity, you must not give him anything."

"I have taken a vow of charity," said the king sternly. "I thank you for your concern, but I cannot refuse a request for help. I cannot break my vow."

"But he will ruin you!" Shukracharya said. "He will take everything. Your kingdom, your wealth, your power!"

"I cannot break my vow," the king repeated. "As my teacher, it is your duty to help me keep my word."

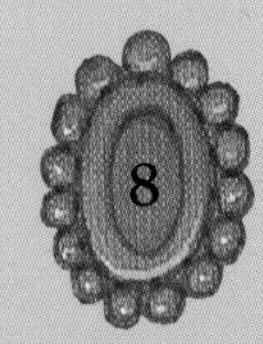

Years passed. Vamana grew into a strong little boy, and then a brilliant young man. Finally the day came when he was ready to visit Bali. He traveled to the court to see the king.

"What brings you here, young man?" asked Bali, looking down at the dwarf with some amusement.

"A simple request, O King," said the visitor. "My parents are very poor. I am a student with no money and no place to live. I need a little piece of land on which to build a small cottage." When he finished speaking, a hush fell over the hall. This young dwarf seemed to glow from within. His bright eyes seemed to miss nothing.

"That is all?" asked Bali. "How much land are you asking for?"

"Only as much as I can measure in three steps," said the small stranger. With that statement, a ripple of laughter spread throughout the court. "What could you possibly measure with those short legs of yours? You'll have to build a very small cottage indeed!" the courtiers teased. The dwarf did not seem to take offence—instead, he joined in the general merriment. Soon almost everyone in the court was laughing.

But Shukracharya saw the devious smile on the dwarf's lips. He knew there must be a hidden trick, and he watched warily as the king asked for the ceremonial water jug that was used before all acts of charity. *Somehow, I must stop him!* he thought. *The king must not proceed with this gift!* Quick as a wink Shukracharya turned himself into a little fly and wedged himself tightly in the spout of the water jug. *If the king cannot pour water, the ritual cannot be completed,* he told himself, with a triumphant little shake of his wings.

But the dwarf, whose eyes missed nothing, had seen the guru's transformation. "The pot seems to be stuck," he said to the king. "Allow me to clear it for you." He poked the spout with a twig. Out flew Shukracharya, buzzing frantically—the twig had poked him right in the eyes.

The king went ahead with the ceremony. He sipped from the jug three times, chanting the mantra that accompanies an act of charity, and then said, "Now, if you please, you may take three steps to measure out your land."

He turned to look down at the dwarf. But to his astonishment the dwarf now towered over him. Everyone looked up in wonder as the dwarf continued to grow, his head now lost in the clouds, now hiding the moon, his arms now encircling the sun, and now collecting the stars. He continued growing until no one was able to see the beginning or the end of him. He was everywhere. And then they heard a booming voice, calling from all around. "King Bali, in one step I have covered the entire Earth. In my second step I have measured Heaven. What shall I measure now?"

King Bali had learned his lesson. Very humbly, he bowed. "Lord, please place your third step on my head. It is all I have left to offer." The pearls in the king's golden crown shimmered, and his downcast eyes shone with tears.

Lord Vishnu recognized the true humility of King Bali's words. "Thank you," he said. "I promise I will always watch over you." Then Lord Vishnu took his third step, placing his foot on the bent head of King Bali and pressing gently. Slowly the king sank deep into the earth, down and still deeper down, all the way to the Kingdom of the Lower Realms, where he would rule forever, under Lord Vishnu's everlasting protection.

The world was filled with new life. People's spirits rose as they realized they were freed from the demon's long rule and the gods were delighted to return to their homes in Heaven.

There was new life in the heavens as well. When Lord Vishnu took his second step over Heaven, Lord Brahma had taken the chance to pour water over Vishnu's big toe, catching the drops in the small jug he carried with him. One day soon after, he saw a tiny baby girl swimming and diving in the water. Lord Brahma scooped her out and placed her on his palm. "My child, do you know you have in you the divine energy of Lord Vishnu?" he whispered to her tenderly. "My precious one, I will name you Ganga and raise you as my own."

Ganga grew graceful and sweet and gave much joy to all who knew her. Her father Lord Brahma and all the other gods of Heaven adored her. She had a gay and lighthearted sense of humor and laughed easily—sometimes, perhaps, too easily!

Alas, one day her lighthearted laughter got her into deep trouble. When Ganga was still a little girl, Sage Durvasa came to visit Heaven. Unlike Ganga, Sage Durvasa was not known for his sense of humor. On the contrary, he was famous for his ill temper and powerful curses, and anyone who met him was very cautious not to make him angry. One day as he was out walking, he bumped into Pavan, the invisible God of Wind. Pavan's powerful gusts caught Sage Durvasa in a small whirlwind that blew around and around him until, to Durvasa's great dismay, all his clothes began to blow right off him! He clutched at his shawl, but every time he wrapped it around him the wind would tug it right off again. Try as he might, the surly sage could not gather his clothes together. After all, who can catch the wind? The gods knew enough to turn their faces away. Even if they were amused, they had the sense not to show it. But little Ganga had no sense. She pointed and laughed gaily.

Sage Durvasa could not stand to be made fun of. Grimly hanging on to his clothes, he wheeled around in terrible anger. "Girl, you need to learn proper manners. You are a disgrace to Heaven. You mock the saints! You have no place here! You must leave! You must go to Earth as a river," the sage cursed. "When humans wash their dirty clothes in your water, you will realize what a privilege it was to live in Heaven!"

Ganga cried, "Please pardon me. O Sage, I am sorry that I laughed at you. Please, please release me from your curse. I won't misbehave again! I don't want to be a river!"

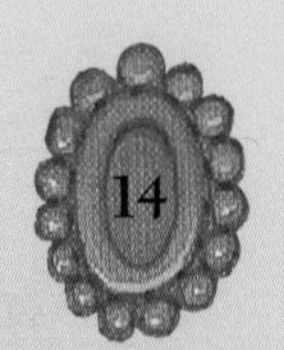

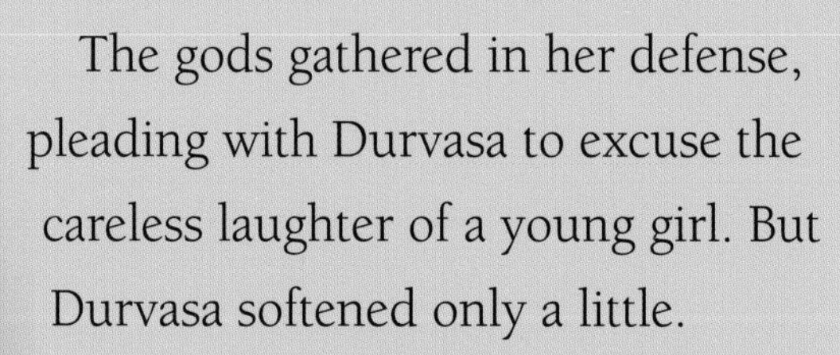

The gods gathered in her defense, pleading with Durvasa to excuse the careless laughter of a young girl. But Durvasa softened only a little.

"I cannot take back what I give," he told Ganga. "I gave you a curse—a well-deserved curse—and you must go to Earth, when you are called. But I see that you are sincerely sorry. I will give you a blessing too. As a river, you will be worshipped as long as you live on Earth. Your water will purify the souls of men and release them from their sins."

Ganga was heartbroken at the thought of leaving her home and friends. All the other gods, too, were shocked and saddened that they would eventually have to lose their darling Ganga. But Ganga had a good heart, and after thinking it over, she realized that she had been given the chance to help ease human sorrows. In turn, this thought eased her own burden of sorrow and even gave her hope as she waited for the moment she would be called to Earth.

That moment was still some years away. On Earth, battles were being won and lost, kingdoms rose and fell, leaders came to power and then were defeated. Of all the leaders, King Sagar was one of the most ambitious. It was his goal to rule the entire planet.

In those times, there was an established custom to avoid unnecessary war. When a king decided to invade a neighboring land, he could send a single powerful horse, accompanied by an army, rather than simply launching a bloody attack. It was understood that people in the neighboring territory could either choose to capture the horse, thus inviting battle, or let the horse alone, thus signaling that they surrendered. So King Sagar sent a powerful steed, decorated with great finery and expensive ornaments, throughout all the territories and countries of the earth. Because the king's power was well known and respected, his horse was never captured. Leaders and citizens from every corner of the earth accepted his rule. When he had conquered Earth, the ambitious king sent the mighty horse galloping toward Heaven.

Needless to say, the king of the gods, Lord Indra, was not at all pleased. He had no desire to be ruled by King Sagar. Lord Indra caught the horse and led it to a desolate marshland. No one was in sight except a holy man, Sage Kapil, who was deep in meditation and did not notice when Lord Indra tied the horse to a tree nearby.

King Sagar's army, made up of his sixty thousand sons, searched high and low, looking for the horse. When they found it near Sage Kapil, they accused the sage of stealing it. "You're a thief! You're only pretending to meditate!" they shouted angrily.

Needless to say, the sage was not at all pleased either. No one likes to be accused wrongly, and he was furious to be so rudely interrupted. When he saw the clamoring army, he shot a ray of white-hot fire at them from his eyes. In a single flash all sixty thousand were burned down to a small pile of ashes.

Meanwhile, King Sagar grew more and more worried as weeks, then months, then entire seasons passed with no news from his army. Finally he sent out his only remaining son, Anshuman, to investigate.

When Anshuman reached the hermitage of Sage Kapil, he learned the terrible news. The horse was still there, grazing under the tree, but all that remained of his sixty thousand brothers was a heap of smoldering ash. "Your brothers have been consumed by my yoga fire, and their spirits are trapped," said the sage. "Only the holiest of water can purify them. You must ask Lord Brahma to send Ganga to Earth. She was born of water that touched the holy feet of Vishnu. Only she can wash the ash and release the souls of your brothers." Sage Kapil handed Anshuman the reins of the horse. "Your horse is safe. Take him and go back to your father."

Anshuman thanked the sage respectfully and returned with a heavy heart to his father. The king was overcome with grief to hear the fate of his many sons. He gave his crown to Anshuman and went into the forest alone to pray. "Oh Brahma, please release the souls of my sons!" But there was no answer from the gods, and within a short time the old king died of a broken heart.

When Anshuman became old, he, too, handed over the throne to his son and went into the woods to pray to Lord Brahma. And he, too, failed to get a response from Heaven. Like his father before him, he died a sad old man. His son followed in his footsteps, and his son's son after him, and so on through many generations, each king dying in lonely and unanswered prayer in the forest.

Then finally, in the seventh generation, Prince Bhagirath broke the hopeless cycle. Unlike the kings before him, Bhagirath did not wait to grow old before dedicating himself to a life of prayer. Instead, he gave up his power and wealth when he was a young man and went into the forest to live a life of purity and prayer. He sat beneath a tree, meditating

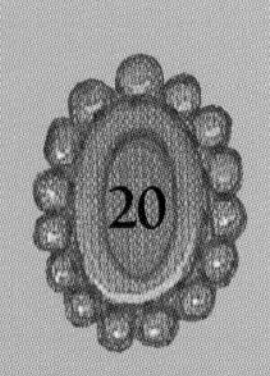

piously, and in time he came to resemble the figure of a holy man, with a long beard and a glowing aura. And unlike the kings before him, Bhagirath found that his prayers were answered.

Pleased with the young prince's sacrifice and determination, Lord Brahma appeared to him and asked, "What do you desire, son?"

"Lord Brahma, I beg of you to send your daughter Ganga to Earth. The spirits of my ancestors are trapped in a mound of smoldering ash. Only Ganga can set them free." Bhagirath spoke with great humility and reverence, which impressed Brahma.

"I will ask Ganga to go to Earth," Lord Brahma replied. "But if I let her go wild, her power would be uncontrollable. She would overwhelm the earth with flooding and destruction. First you must pray to Lord Shiva to restrain her," Lord Brahma said, and then he disappeared into the sky above.

Bhagirath began another long and difficult time of prayer. Standing balanced on the tiptoe of his left foot, his right leg bent and his hands together, he closed his eyes and repeated the mantra to call Shiva. He became so completely absorbed in his prayer that he didn't even realize when Shiva arrived.

"Open your eyes," Lord Shiva said to him in a rumbling voice. "You have done well. I will be happy to help you."

As Bhagirath watched in awe, Shiva let his hair loose. He shook his head once and his matted locks spread out and covered the entire earth like a veil of dark and shimmering silk. "Ask Ganga to come now," he said.

Ganga, taking the form of a river, cascaded down from the heavens in a wild torrent. A swirling stream of shining water connected Heaven to Earth—but only for an instant. Then Ganga fell into the net of hair Lord Shiva had cast for her. With one fluid motion, Shiva gathered his hair in a giant knot on the top of his head, trapping the river Ganga within.

Then Shiva sat down right where he was and resumed the meditation he had interrupted to answer Bhagirath's prayer. He stared straight ahead and didn't pay any attention to Ganga, who waved her arms and screamed, "Set me free! Set me free!" Shiva didn't pay any more attention to Bhagirath, either. Bhagirath was confused and upset. He knew that it would be impolite to bother Lord Shiva when he was meditating. But how could Ganga help his ancestors when she was trapped in Shiva's hair? Finally, in desperation, he blurted, "Lord Shiva, we need Ganga on Earth. Please, have mercy on my poor ancestors. Please, Lord Shiva, let her loose!"

Once more, Lord Shiva heard him. He squeezed one of his locks and Ganga came rushing out again, but not as wildly. "Follow the prince," Shiva said, and he vanished into thin air. Bhagirath was elated, and Ganga bubbled with pleasure to be free, as she dropped from the icy peaks and valleys of the Himalayas. Down and down she flowed, following Bhagirath, who walked ahead blowing a conch shell. As the melting snows from the mountains joined her, she grew ever deeper and wider.

By the time they reached the plains of northern India, Ganga was a huge river, though she herself did not yet recognize how great she had become. One day as she followed Bhagirath past a holy hermitage, she heard the chants of Sage Janu and his students. She stopped briefly to listen to the lovely singing and did not notice that her banks overflowed as if stopped by a dam. She did not realize what havoc she was creating. Monks and students fled the rapidly rising water, and the sacred pots used in worship floated away. The river continued to rise, flooding temples and houses.

Sage Janu, a wise man indeed, understood just what was happening. *Ganga has come from Heaven,* he thought. *She doesn't know her own powers. There is only one thing to do.* He quickly chanted a mantra and then took a long sip of the raging waters. The flood subsided. The river vanished. All that remained were the drenched students, the sacred pots scattered about the courtyard, and a dry riverbed.

Bhagirath, walking ahead, turned his head at the sudden silence. Where was Ganga? Where was the mighty river? He ran back to the hermitage. "Ganga, Ganga, where are you?" he called frantically.

Sage Janu was sitting peacefully under a tree. "Here she is," he said, rubbing his enormous belly. "She has no self control," he said with a satisfied burp. "She needed to learn some respect."

Bhagirath flung himself on the ground. "Please release her," he said. "I have struggled so hard to bring her to Earth!" In desperation he narrated the long, sad story of his sixty thousand ancestors, how they died, and how they were cursed, their spirits trapped in their own ashes. He told the sage of his years of solitary prayer and penance, of his meetings with Brahma and Shiva. "Please, let her go. Earth needs her now."

The sage was moved by the tale and by Bhagirath's deep sincerity. "I will help you, of course," he said. "Here she is," he said, and right away gouged a deep cut in his thigh. Bhagirath stared in wonder. Instead of blood, Ganga poured from the wound, clear and pure. She had calmed her exuberance and was wiser from the experience of being swallowed up. Happily, the two thanked the sage, who blessed them as they set off again on their journey.

Everywhere they went, the earth responded with new life. Everything Ganga touched was renewed by her goodness: flowers opened in a rainbow of blossoms, crops grew lush and green, and throngs of people came to bathe, chanting praises, offering prayers for their ancestors, their spirits renewed and purified by her pure waters.

Ganga and Bhagirath traveled all the way across India and reached the desolate marshlands at the far eastern shores of India, where they found Sage Kapil. The old man was delighted to see them. "I have waited many, many years for this day," he said. He led Ganga to the heap of ashes—all that remained of the army. As Ganga poured her waters through the ashes, the spirits of the sixty thousand brothers emerged, lit up with divine light. Bhagirath was filled to the brim with joy. At last, the souls of his ancestors were free! The spirit beings rose like a luminous cloud, offering prayers to Ganga and showering Bhagirath with flowers as they ascended to the heavens above. And Ganga, too, was filled with joy. She had found her purpose on Earth. She was truly needed.

From that day, humans have continued to come to Ganga for help. Her sacred waters are believed to contain the energy of Lords Brahma, Vishnu, and Shiva and to have the power to release the human spirit from pain and despair. Thousands of hermitages, temples, shrines, and sacred sites have sprung up along her banks over the many thousands of years since her journey first began. Millions of people worship her, traveling great distances to bathe in her water, bringing her their woes, seeking her comfort.

So Ganga, the river goddess who made the long journey from Heaven to Earth, is still a wondrous and mighty river, flowing from the highest peaks of the Himalayas down to the Bay of Bengal. She continues to make the long journey every day. And because she touches the lives of all who come to worship her, listening to their troubles, easing their pain, and washing away their sins, her journey is still filled with tales of sorrow and joy, hardship and renewed hope.

A Note to Parents and Teachers

This story, peopled by gods, kings, and demons, is actually about the values that empower regular human beings. Though he is a demon, King Bali is highly disciplined and generous to his own subjects. His virtues have earned him enough power to kick the less-disciplined gods out of Heaven, but too much power weakens Bali's character.

He falls when he allows mockery to cloud his judgment. When Lord Vishnu approaches his court in the guise of Vamana, the whole court mocks him, leading Bali to discount his teacher's warnings and underestimate the dwarf. As a result, he loses his entire kingdom. Mockery costs little Ganga her joyful life in Heaven, too. She earns the curse of becoming a river on Earth by mocking Sage Durvasa. And the sixty thousand sons of King Sagar are turned into a heap of ash for mocking an innocent man—Sage Kapil.

In contrast, Prince Bhagirath's humility and determination help him succeed in his mission to bring Ganga out of Heaven to release the souls of his ancestors. He is remembered to this day as a humble man whose strength of character and perseverance earned their just reward.

About the Illustrations

Harish Johari and Pieter Weltevrede created the illustrations with watercolor and tempera paints. Using transparent watercolors, the artists painted each picture in several steps. After outlining the figures, they filled them in, using three tones for each color to achieve a three-dimensional effect; next they applied the background colors. After each step they "fixed" the painting by rinsing it with water until only the paint absorbed by the silk remained.

Then the artists applied a "wash," using opaque tempera paints. After wetting the painting again, they applied the tempera to the surface until the whole painting appeared to be behind a colored fog. While the wash was still wet, they used a dry brush to remove it from the faces, hands, and feet of the figures. They let the wash dry completely, then rinsed the silk again to fix the colors. To achieve the desired color and emotional tone, each painting received several washes and fixes. Finally, the artists redefined the delicate line work of each piece, allowing the painting to reemerge from within the clouds of wash.

Please feel free to trace or photocopy this drawing of Ganga for children to color.